HIGH JACKED & THE STRANGER

HIGH JACKED & THE STRANGER

BOB CUCINO

High Jacked
&
The Stranger
Bob Cucino

All rights reserved
Copyright © 2023 Bob Cucino
No part of this publication may be reproduced, distributed, or transmitted in
any form or by any means, including photocopying, recording, or other
electronic or mechanical methods, without the prior written permission of the
publisher, except in the case of brief quotations embodied in critical reviews
and certain other noncommercial uses permitted by copyright law.

Published by BooxAI
ISBN: 978-965-578-474-9

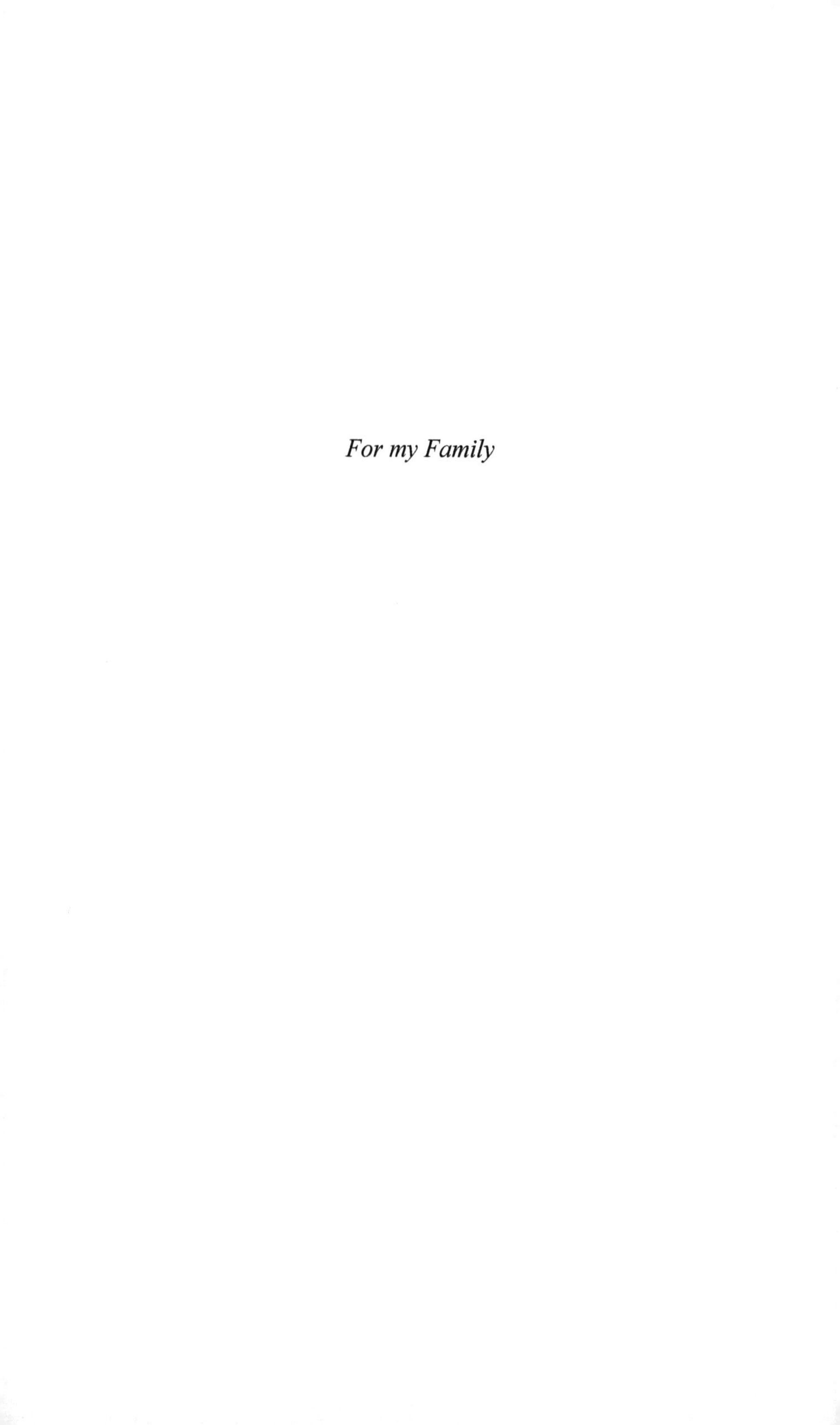

For my Family

PART I

HIGH JACKED

1

———————

I t's mid-October and the cruise ship "Spirit Of The Sea" is on its last leg of their around the world voyage about 150 miles off the east coast of Africa. The ship "Spirit Of The Sea" is one of the newest ships belonging to the Arastolo Group out of Greece. This is its second around the world voyage. The ship can carry approximately 3300 passengers and a crew of 175.

The passengers were entertained as soon as they stepped on board. The captain greeted the passengers as they boarded and also gave him a chance to meet them one on one.

There was entertainment day and night. Food on all eight decks. So much to do and many choices and all hard to choose.

Every two to three nights at sea the fourth night would dock at a different port so the passengers could spend the next day shopping and visiting the different countries.

By the time they reached the final leg of the voyage, the passengers could not ask for anything more. It was an enjoyable voyage. New friends have been made and longtime relationships have begun. It has been a voyage to remember.

It's now early morning and the sun is coming up. A lot of the passengers have finished their breakfast and are already taking their morning walkabout. The walkabout is when the passengers stroll around the ship's decks and admire the view on all sides of the ship. This morning the passengers were entertained by a school of hunchback whales. There must have been 15 to 20 of them jumping out of the water and splashing as their heavy bodies slammed the water. It was a sight that they would never forget. It was like these whales orchestrated all the movements together as one. The passengers just watched in awe. Too bad they didn't see what else was being orchestrated.

2

THE UNKNOWN

All the passengers were watching the whales on the Port Side of the Cruise Ship, but what they didn't see were 5 small speed boats with armed Somalian Pirates approaching fast and seemed not to be noticed. At fifty yards from the ship one of the passengers noticed the pirate boats coming toward the ship. The passenger alerted one of the crew. When the crewman noticed what was happening, he immediately contacted the captain. The captain sounded the alert horn and contacted authorities of the impending danger from the approaching pirates. The authorities acknowledged the captain's distress call. Before the Captain or the authorities could reply, shots were fired from the Pirate boats at the radio antennas on the ship which knocked out all communications. The Pirates are already at the side of the cruise ship and throwing grapple hooks onto the ship. The Pirates climb the ropes and in a matter of minutes, fifteen of the Pirates are on the deck of the ship. Firing their guns into the air and by this time the passengers are in a panic. Several of the passengers developed chest pains and one had a fatal heart attack.

By this time each of the eight decks of the cruise ship had eight heavily armed pirates on board.

Each group of pirates gathered all the passengers and had them moved into what was the auditorium. Within an hour, all decks were under the control of the Pirates.

Eight more pirates made their way to the bridge. On the way up to the bridge, some of the crew tried to stop the Pirates. One of the Pirates shot the crewman another hit the other crewman at the back of the head and he fell to the floor unconscious.

They make it to the bridge and the captain is waiting for them. As they enter the bridge, one of the Pirates walks over to the captain where he was standing next to the controls. The pirate walks up to him and with one hit from the butt of a rifle to his head, the captain falls to the floor unconscious; his second mate attempts to help the Captain and is shot in the arm by one of the Pirates.

The pirate who seemed to be the leader told the others on the bridge. This ship is now OURS and we are holding it hostage.

He yells to the radio man YOU call your boss. The radio man says we have no communication, you shot out our communication antenna. The pirate hands him a GPS phone that is linked to a satellite and can make calls anywhere in the world.

The first mate bleeding from the bullet shot in the leg grabs the phone and calls the main dispatch and tells them what has happened and the Pirates have taken over the ship.

Dispatch asks about the passengers. The mate tells dispatch how all the passengers are corralled on the rack deck. We have several casualties. The Pirate then speaks up. Give me the phone. The pirate says to the Dispatch on the other end of the phone and gives his demands. The dispatch asks what your name is. Why do you want my name?

Because I would like to know if I have to meet your demands, I should at least know who I am talking to. The pirate agrees and says You call me Ariko. Ok, Ariko, what are your demands? I want $100 million US Dollars. I want them dropped off on the top deck of this ship. I want this done in no more than 48 hours. Dispatch says to Ariko that it is such short notice to get that much money up in just 48 hours. YOU listen to me, Mr. Dispatch. If you do not meet my demands at the end of 48 hours, we will execute a passenger for each day that goes by. DO I MAKE MYSELF CLEAR?!!! He yells into the phone. Dispatch says to keep the line free and hangs up.

Ariko says to the crew I'm not afraid to die, but many of you will die before me.

Meanwhile back at Greece headquarters.

 Scotland Yard and the US Government have been notified. Scotland Yard shares information on this Ariko, who is a familiar name and has been wanted by many European Countries and by the US government.

The US Government has been in touch with Naval Intelligence since the first call went out before the antennas were shot down.

Naval Intelligence tells the joint chiefs of staff what is in the area...

3

FIRST THINGS FIRST

The first plan of action is to find out what naval ships are in the area equipped for this type of rescue mission. According to Naval Intelligence, there is one aircraft carrier with a Marine attachment. A Battleship with Navy Seals / Special Forces and one of the New Titan Submarines. All three ships are approximately   Seventeen hours away. In the meantime, the Chief Joints of Staff begin a conference call to plan the rescue. Meanwhile Scotland Yard is working with the Greek ship owners regarding the raising of the $100 million.

Back on the cruise ship the captain is picked up and put in a chair. The First Mate is taken care of by the Ships Doctor. The bullet that was shot at the First Mate's leg.

Luckily went right through the leg. The Doctor cleans the wound and bandages the leg. Ariko, who is the self, claimed leader of the Pirates speaks good English. He is tall, slender, not the muscular type. Curly bushy hair, large teeth with one of the front ones missing. Walking back and forth on the bridge as if he was a new father to be or it could even fear that he may have bit off more than he can chew. He keeps looking out the windows of the bridge and sees an oil tanker heading towards them. The Tanker is trying to radio the cruise ship and when the Tanker realizes the radio is working, they try Morse Code with the lights. Ariko yells, "what are they doing" he asks the Captain? The Captain says "they are asking if we are ok ?" Ariko says you tell them we are ok. The captain tells the radio operator to send the Tanker a message that we are ok and just sightseeing. With a wink in his eye, the radio operator knew what he had to do. The Radioman signaled the Tanker that they were under siege and to stay clear. Two passengers were murdered. The Tanker will stand by and radio the Coast Guard. The Radioman acknowledges. What did you tell them Ariko asks. The radioman says we are letting the passengers watch the whales. Ok, Ariko says. The first 24 hours pass and now Ariko starts telling the Captain this time tomorrow if we do not have the money, I shoot one passenger. The captain replies my company is doing everything they can to raise the money. Ariko says at Noon you call your boss and tell him I am going to pick out the first passenger to shoot tomorrow.

The Captain of the Tanker notifies the Coast Guards. They put the Captain of the Tanker in touch with Naval Intelligence. The captain relays the message he received from the Cruise Ship. Naval Intelligence asks how close they are to the Cruise ship. The captain says they are about five hundred yards away. General Dwayne Jackson of Naval Intelligence asked the Captain of the Tanker. Can you anchor there? I could understand why he asked? The General tells the Captain that his ship can aid in the rescue attempt to free the ship from the Pirates. The captain agrees. What if the cruise ship radios back to ask why aren't we moving. The General says "tell them you have engine trouble and are in the process of correcting the problem." Both men agree.

The General informs the captain of the tanker that at 00:40 there will be the Tioga Nuclear Submarine surface on the side of the tanker where a team of Navy Seals will come aboard your ship for debarkation. Both men end their conversation. Twelve hours and counting before the first passenger is to be executed. General Jackson contacts the rest of the Chiefs of Staff and goes over the rescue. The General informs Naval Defense to have the Navy Seals that are on the battleship USS GW Bush to transfer to the Titan Seahawk submarine and rendezvous with the oil tank anchored five hundred yards off the cruise ship's port side.

Time now 00:40 and the Sub surfaces along the side of the Tanker out of the sight of the cruise ship. The crew of the Tanker has never seen a submarine surface from out of nowhere and what is more right alongside the Tanker. The Sub ties up alongside the Tanker. The Seals team, which amount to about fifteen navy seals, climb on board the oil tanker. The captain is there to greet them. Whatever you need us to do, we are at your service.

The seals set up communications. Each seal has a waterproof radio phone. They are also equipped with an arsenal that could destroy a small city. All plans are ready and are now about to be implemented.

4

———————

Seal Team 1 sets up two Snipers on the Oil Tanker. These expert snipers can hit a target 2 miles away. Their mission is to eliminate any of the Pirates at any time necessary.

Seal Team 2 consists of 8 Seals. All are equipped with underwater air tanks and rubber suits for the underwater swim to the cruise ship.

The Seals debark from the Tanker from the opposite side of the cruise ship, so they are not noticed by any of the Pirates from the cruise ship.

As Seal Team 2 makes their way underwater to the cruise ship, the Snipers use their rifle scopes to scan the ship for activity by the Pirates. As Seal Team 1 reaches the cruise ship Seal Team 2 communicates with Seal Team 1 and gives them an update on the activity going on the ship. Team 2 is told the safest area to board the ship is the Aft of the ship and go in through the propeller maintenance hatch door. Team 2 makes it to the hatch and manages to open it and Team 2 is all on board in the engine room. They remove all their scuba gear and move as planned.

They know through heat sensors where all the passengers are located. They reach the first deck and the room with the passengers. Silently, Team 2 eliminates the Pirates on deck one. They instruct the passengers to stay together and not to leave the room.

As Team 2 moves its way to deck 2, they encounter 3 Pirates in the hall next to the entrance to the room where the second deck passengers are. One of the Pirates sees one of the Seals and quickly grabs a passenger and, with a knife, holds it to her throat. The Pirate starts to yell at the other Pirates in the room which were 4 altogether. The other Pirates run up to the pirate holding the girl. The pirate holding the girl tells the other Pirates about the seal he saw. They start to scramble to look for the Seal when there was a sound Pop, pop, Pop. The last pop was a shot in the head of the pirate holding the girl. The pops were gunshots from the Snipers who were on the Oil Tanker. Team 1 confirms to Team 2 that all is secured. Team 2 rushes in and calms the passengers down. They tell the passengers the same thing they told the passengers on deck 1. The Seals remove the bodies of the dead Pirates to another room.

As the Seals move to deck 3, they face another obstacle. There is a Pirate at the top of the stairway, another near the elevator and another pirate at the far end of another elevator. Team 2 has to get the Pirates together. They come up with a plan to distract the pirate watching the room and hopefully will get the attention of the others.

The Seal Team starts a smoke bomb in a closet at the bottom of the stairway below where the Pirate is standing. The pirate sees and smells smoke at the bottom of the stairway and goes to check it out. When he reaches the bottom of the stairway and opens the closet door, one of the seals grabs him and holds a knife to his throat.

The Seal tells the pirate to call the other Pirates to come quickly. One by one, they all came running for they also see the smoke, not knowing what was waiting for them.

As each pirate came, each one was subdued, bound and gagged. Once again, the Seals give the passengers the same instructions as the others.

Decks 5 and 6 were met with less resistance. The Pirates were overtaken by the passengers, so when the Seal Team came in, the Pirates were on the floor. Looked like the passengers gave the Pirates one hell of a beaten then tied them up.

The passengers all yelled with joy When the Seals came in.

The Seals move to deck 7. As they approach the passengers on deck 7 who walk out but Ariko with a male passenger in his fifties. They could hear his wife would be screaming and crying for he was to be the first passenger to be executed. Ariko says to one of the 4 other Pirates who came down to the lower deck to get the passenger.

You go to the other decks and make sure everything is ok.

Team 2 Seals were waiting for the Pirate Ariko sent to check on the others on the lower decks. In seconds the pirate never did the task Ariko asked him to do.

The Seals returned to the room where the passengers were on deck 7. There were two Pirates in the room who were easily subdued. They were tied and gagged and locked in a closet.

The Seal team makes it to the 8th deck and part of this deck is the Bridge where Ariko and his 6 other Pirates held the captain and his crew along with the passenger, soon to be executed.

Ariko commands the radioman to call his boss. He calls the shipping company dispatch. The radioman begins to talk to dispatch when Ariko grabs the phone. Your time is up and because you did not bring me my money, this passenger is going to die. His death will be on your conscious. You could hear the passenger sobbing heavily and saying I don't want to die. Please don't kill me and sobs louder. I have a family he goes on. Ariko yells into the phone, "Do You hear how?" he cries. His death is on your hands and there will be another passenger executed tomorrow if I do not get my Money and hangs up the phone. The Pirates have their guns on the Captain and crew while Ariko pulls out his revolver and puts his pistol to the passenger's head, he cocks the trigger then pop, pop, pop. The Captain looks expecting to see a dead passenger, but in the end, are the dead Pirates. Three were shot from the Oil Tanker and the others were taken out by Team 2.

Soon the battleship GW Bush was alongside the cruise ship. The cruise ship looked like a rubber raft next to the battleship. A special team came aboard to remove all the Pirates' dead ones and those who were lucky to still be alive.

As for the Seal Team, they disappeared just as fast as they appeared.

The captain took control of his ship and it wasn't long before they were heading home. The passengers had the option of leaving the ship by helicopter and being taken to the nearest Port, where the shipping company would arrange transportation home.

Only a few opted for that option. The rest had too much to talk about to their new friends and wanted to finish the cruise.

The End

PART II

THE STRANGER

CHAPTER 1

Katie was getting dressed because she had to catch the Red Eye to Chicago but she was running late cause she got stuck in the elevator of her apartment building. Unbeknown to her, she was not the only one that was stuck in the elevator. Someone she did not know but soon she would and regret the adventure she would soon endure.

Stay Tuned

Katie was rushing around, trying to get her clothes packed so she could leave for the airport. The weather was not cooperating also. It was pouring rain and lightning and thunder. The thunder was so loud that it shook her apartment. The Lightning would light up the whole street. Katie was determined to make that flight. She was almost finished packing when there came a knock at the door. She looked through her security peephole that was in the door but did not see anyone there. So, she went back to packing. What Katie didn't realize was that when she went to the door, she unlocked it and forgot that she did. Now Katie is in her bedroom finishing up. As she was locking her suitcase a bolt of lightning flashed at her window that made her jump but what the flash of lightning also did was show a shadow lurking in the room and as she was about to scream...

CHAPTER 2

Katie was about to scream when all of a sudden, she was grabbed from behind and a cloth which was soaked with "Ether". In case you didn't know Ether is used to render a person unconscious. Katie fell to her knee. When she awoke, she didn't know where she was. The room was dark, and she was dizzy and sick to her stomach. Her hands were tied behind her and her legs were tied. It seemed like she was knocked out for hours. She lay on a cold cement floor and there was a moldy smell in the room. She tried to free herself, but the ropes were too tight. By this time, she was cold and thirsty. She felt her throat closing and a panic feeling started to overtake her. She tried to think happy thoughts to calm herself and relieve her panic feeling. She was perspiring and filled with fear. Not knowing what happened and who did this to her. Her imagination running wild; by this time she is thinking to herself... Am I going to die? She kept asking herself. She begins to cry and thinks to herself this must be a dream. This can't be happening to me. This only happens in the movies. More time had gone by and Katie had no idea what time it was. Just then, she heard a scratching sound coming from a wall. Oh my God, she says it must be a rat and the sound of the scratching makes her think that this must be a...

A Big Rat. She could almost feel the rat scratching and coming through the wall. Am I going to be rat bait, she thought. Trying to move and loosen the ropes but to no avail. Suddenly Katie hears what sounds like a door opening. As she tried to turn and look, she felt a kick to the stomach. Katie, now in great pain, vomits all over herself.

CHAPTER 3

She began to cry and yell at her assailant whom she could not see. Why are you doing this to me? in a high screeching voice. Why, why she kept saying over and over. Suddenly her assailant grabbed her hair and pulled her up so she could see his face. It's YOU! You're the Janitor. Why are you doing this to me? She screamed? He looked her in the eyes and tells her you are my ticket out of this God forsaken place. Katie looks at him with disbelief. I don't understand. The Janitor says I am going to make a lot of money on you. He goes on to say "I sold you to the highest bidder." WHAT!!!!! You heard me, he went on to say. I find beautiful young girls and I sell them to Very Rich Buyers from all over and what they with you is no concern of mine. A cold chill went up Katie's spine. This guy is a freak, she says to herself. I must get out of here... but how. She keeps thinking and knows if she doesn't try, she will be lost forever. If only I had a way out. Katie starts to put a plan together. Katie turns to the Janitor, who looks like someone from the Walking Dead. He had long stringy hair. He had an unshaven beard and he reeked with such a smell and missing teeth that made his breath horrendous. As she tried to compose herself, she said to him if I am to stay healthy for you to make your money, you had better get me some food and water. As the Janitor looked at his prisoner, he thought to himself and figured he had better get her some food for the Buyers would not think too kindly the way he handles their merchandise. They would have no problem slicing his throat. He turns to Katie and tells her he will go get her some food.

CHAPTER 4

As he leaves the storage room, he shuts the lights and locks the door. Katie lays on the floor and remembers looking around the room when the lights were on.

She remembers that room was the janitor's storage room in the apartment building. She remembers there was some type of workbench that seemed to have tools on it. Somehow, she has to get to that bench. She began to roll on the floor. Trying to remember exactly where the bench was but it was so dark, she kept ending up in the wrong spot. Finally, somehow her leg got caught on the part of the bench. As she moved her legs up the side of the bench, she caught her leg on a nail and cut herself.

She began to put the ropes that were on her tied legs on the point of the nail and tried to rip the rope apart.

Again, she hears that scratching sound coming from the wall, only this time where she lays on the floor. The scratching was so loud that it seemed it was coming right from the wall next to where she lays her head. It's a known fact that rats can smell blood 500 yards away. By now, Katie's leg is loaded with blood not so much from her first encounter with the nail but with all the attempts to remove the ropes from her legs which are now covered in blood and are all on the floor. The scratching is getting louder and louder. Now Katie is trying frantically to loosen the ropes when the scratching seemed like it made a little hole in the wall right near her head. Katie keeps saying please God, please God, let me get out of this and I promise I will go to church every Sunday. The scratching was so loud it seemed like the rat had made an opening, but it still wasn't big enough to get through.

Suddenly Katie managed to get the ropes on her legs loose and managed to free her legs. She managed to get up and free her hands. As she stood next to the bench, her hand touched a pipe that was on the bench.

Just then, she heard the door start to open.

CHAPTER 5

The room was still dark and Katie, with a pipe in her hand and ready to swing away as soon as that door opened. The door slowly opens a pinch of light starts to shine through. Katie regrips the pipe, ready to swing as if she was going to hit a Grand Slam. The door opens and as he walks in, Katie swings away. Her assailant goes flying into the air. Katie drops the pipe and stands over her assailant with shock and bewilderment. For you see, it wasn't the Janitor. It was Jason, her finance. Lying next to Jason was the Janitor, who was unconscious. Katie falls to her knees to comfort her unconscious finance' Jason she keeps calling his name. Finally, he starts to awaken and looks at Katie while holding his bleeding head. Katie puts her arms around Jason and apologizes. Was that you that hit me What's going on? What happened to you? As she went to explain what happened she felt a knocking on her leg. As she looked down in disbelief, she and Jason had a look of horror on their face as he…

CHAPTER 6

Jason looked down in disbelief. He saw a rat the size of a cat licking up the blood that had been bleeding from Katie's leg. With one shove to push Katie out of the way Jason gives a swift kick to the rat that was about to take a chunk out of Katie's leg. That rat went flying in the air as if Jason was going for one of his famous field goals. Oh, I did not mention Jason plays football for the New York Giants as their field Goalkicker and is also the fiancé of Katie.

Katie jumps into Jason's arms and holds him and gives kiss after kiss after kiss. She was about to ask. What are you doing when?

She immediately Stops and screams to the Janitor where is he? Where is he? But before she could finished, she sees the Janitor on the floor in a pool of blood and you can imagine where that Big Rat ended up. Katie filled in with questions for Jason when the police showed up. Jason tells the police what happened, as Katie listens. Jason goes on to say that he was waiting for Katie at the Airport and when she didn't arrive, he became concerned and tried calling Katie, but there was no answer cause Katie's phone was in her room. When the Janitor took Katie, he left her phone in the room. When Jason got to Katie's apartment and with his key went inside and saw that there was a struggle. He immediately left the room and went down the elevator and met up with the Janitor. A small conversation started and both men ended up down at the janitor's storage room, where an argument started and the next moment, the Janitor lays dead on the floor. That's what happened, officer. Jason says to the officer would it be alright if we leave? The officer says would you like me to call a rescue. Jason No, that's ok. I will take her myself to the hospital. The officer says sure, go ahead. As Jason and Katie start to leave, the officer says ah, Jason, one more thing mind if I ask you another question? Jason stops and slowly turns to face the officer, only this time he was reaching for something in his pocket. When he finally turned to face the officer Jason had a gun in his hand but unbeknown to Jason, the officer had a gun pointing at him. Suddenly shots were fired simultaneously. The officer falls to the floor and Jason lays dead on the floor.

Katie is now in total shock and screaming. Suddenly the hallway is filled with police and rescue people. By the time the Medic sedated Katie to calm her down, both Jason and the Janitor were taken out of the hall. Detective Jill Hargraves goes over to Katie to tell her that they have been watching the Janitor and Jason for quite a while. It seems that Jason is the Kingpin of a girl Trafficking syndication, and the Janitor was an accomplice. They had to wait until they had enough evidence to make an arrest.

Now You Know the Rest Of The Story... The End... Careful who your friends are.